W9-CBI-881

Dear Family and Friends of Young Readers,

Learning to read is one of the most important milestones your child will ever attain. Early reading is hard work, but you can make it easier with Hello Readers.

Just like learning to play a sport or an instrument, learning to read requires many opportunities to work on skills. However, you have to get in the game or experience real music to keep interested and motivated. Hello Readers are carefully structured to provide the right level of text for practice and great stories for experiencing the fun of reading.

Try these activities:

• Reading starts with the alphabet and at the earliest level, you may encourage your child to focus on the sounds of letters in words and sounding out words. With more experienced readers, focus on how words are spelled. Be word watchers!

• Go beyond the book — talk about the story, how it compares with other stories, and what your child likes about it.

• Comprehension — did your child get it? Have your child retell the story or answer questions you may ask about it.

Another thing children learn to do at this age is learn to ride a bike. You put training wheels on to help them in the beginning and guide the bike from behind. Hello Readers help you support your child and then you get to watch them take off as skilled readers.

— Francie Alexander
Chief Academic Officer
Scholastic Education

For Sam, Lizzie, and Bennett
—G.H.

For my dear mother-in-law, Camille,
who is forever young at heart
—B.B.

No part of this publication may be reproduced in whole or in part, or stored in a retrieval system, or transmitted in any form or by any means, electronic, mechanical, photocopying, recording, or otherwise, without written permission of the publisher. For information regarding permission, write to Scholastic Inc., Attention: Permissions Department, 557 Broadway, New York, NY 10012.

ISBN 0-439-44164-1

Text copyright © 2003 by Gail Herman.
Illustrations copyright © 2003 by Bill Basso.
All rights reserved. Published by Scholastic Inc.
SCHOLASTIC, HELLO READER, and associated logos are trademarks
and/or registered trademarks of Scholastic Inc.

12   7 8/0

Printed in the U.S.A.
First printing, May 2003

by Gail Herman
illustrated by Bill Basso

Hello Reader! — Level 2

SCHOLASTIC INC.

New York   Toronto   London   Auckland   Sydney
Mexico City   New Delhi   Hong Kong   Buenos Aires

It was a bright spring day.
Molly was in her backyard.
Trucks were digging.
Workers were shouting.

"Will the pool be ready soon?"
Molly asked.
"Don't worry," said her mom.
"The pool will be ready by the
first day of summer."

Another truck came.
Out came concrete, and more
concrete.
"This will take forever!" said Molly.

Then came tiles.
"Are you sure the pool will be
ready?" asked Molly.
"Yes," said her mom. "It
will be ready by the
first day of summer."

Finally came the water. "Hooray!" shouted Molly. "The pool is ready. And tomorrow is the first day of summer!"

"Call your friends," said her mom.
"Invite them over. You can have
a pool party!"

Molly called Sam, Lizzie, and Ben. "Let's have a pool party tomorrow!" she said.

The next day, Molly woke up early.
"Happy first day of summer!"
she shouted. "Happy pool party!"
She pulled on her bathing suit.

Then she ran downstairs.
"I'm ready for the party!"
she exclaimed.
"Oh, honey," said her dad.
"Look outside."

Molly looked.
Splish, splash.
It was pouring—on the first day
of summer.
"No pool party!" she cried.

Molly felt so bad.
Splish, splash.
Tears as big as raindrops
ran down her cheeks.

"I'm sorry," said her mom.
"But you can still have
a party with your friends."

Molly felt a little better.
She called Sam, Lizzie, and Ben.
"Come over, anyway," she told
them. "We will try to have fun."

When her friends came over,
they wore bathing suits, too.

Molly's mom turned on the
brightest light.
"The sun is so strong!" said Molly.
"I need sunglasses!"

Molly's dad spread a blanket
on the floor.
He brought out apples and oranges,
and sandwiches cut in
little triangles.
"A picnic!" said Molly.

Molly, Sam, Lizzie, and Ben
played tag and hide-and-seek.
"This is almost like being outside,"
said Molly.

She looked out the window.
Splish, splash.
"If only we could go outside—
for real."

"Well," said her dad. "It's not raining as hard."
"And you are wearing bathing suits," said her mom.
"Let's go!" said Molly and her friends.

Molly, Sam, Lizzie, and Ben
ran outside.
Splish! Splash!
They stomped through puddles.
They tried to catch raindrops.

Suddenly, the rain stopped.
The sun peeked out.
Clouds floated away.

"It's sunny!" cried Molly. "Just like
the first day of summer
should be!"
"Ready for a real pool party?"
asked her mom.

Splish! Splash!
Molly swam underwater.
She did handstands.
She kicked and laughed
and jumped around.

"Everyone out of the pool!"
said Molly's dad.
"It is getting late."

"Thank you," said Ben.
"Thanks," said Sam.
"I had a great time," said Lizzie.
"I had a great time, too,"
Molly told her mom.

"The next time it rains, can we have another pool party?" Molly asked.